MW00903162

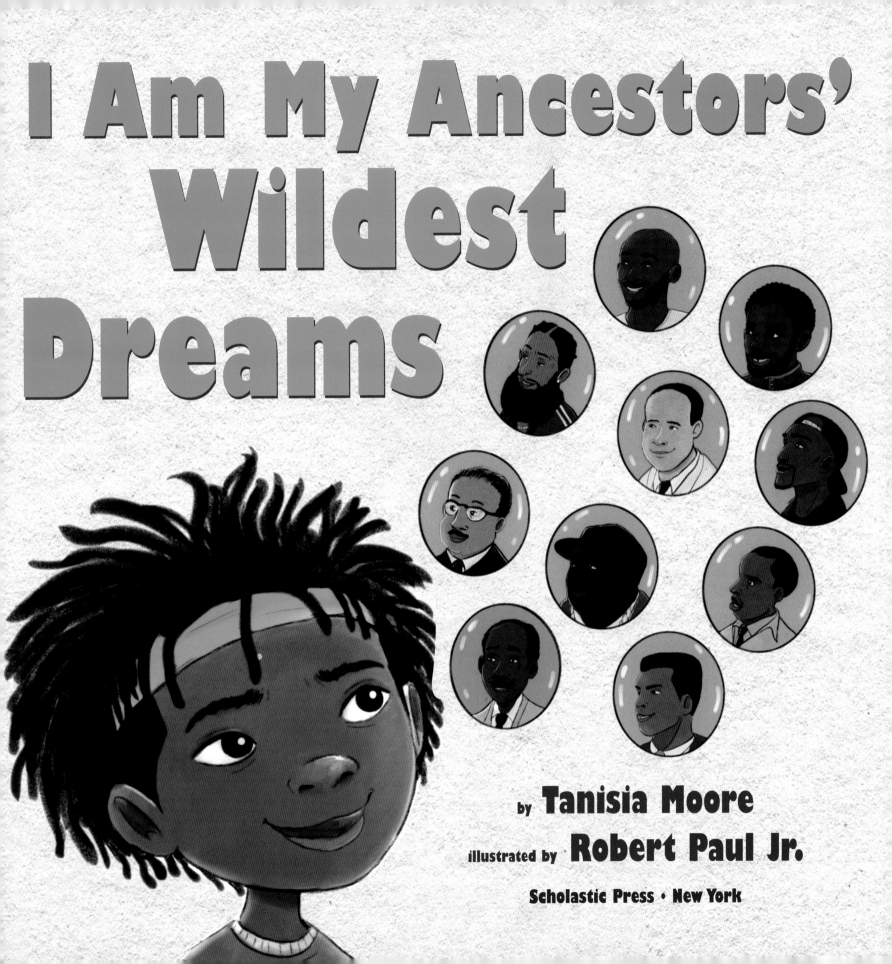

I Am My Ancestors' Wildest Dreams

by Tanisia Moore

illustrated by Robert Paul Jr.

Scholastic Press • New York

I AM FLY.

From my crown down
to the kicks on my feet.
No matter how
I rock my locs,
fro,
or my deep-sea waves . . .

I AM my ancestors' wildest dreams.

When I play with my friends
I love to pretend that I am a KING,
like T'Challa, a BLACK PANTHER.

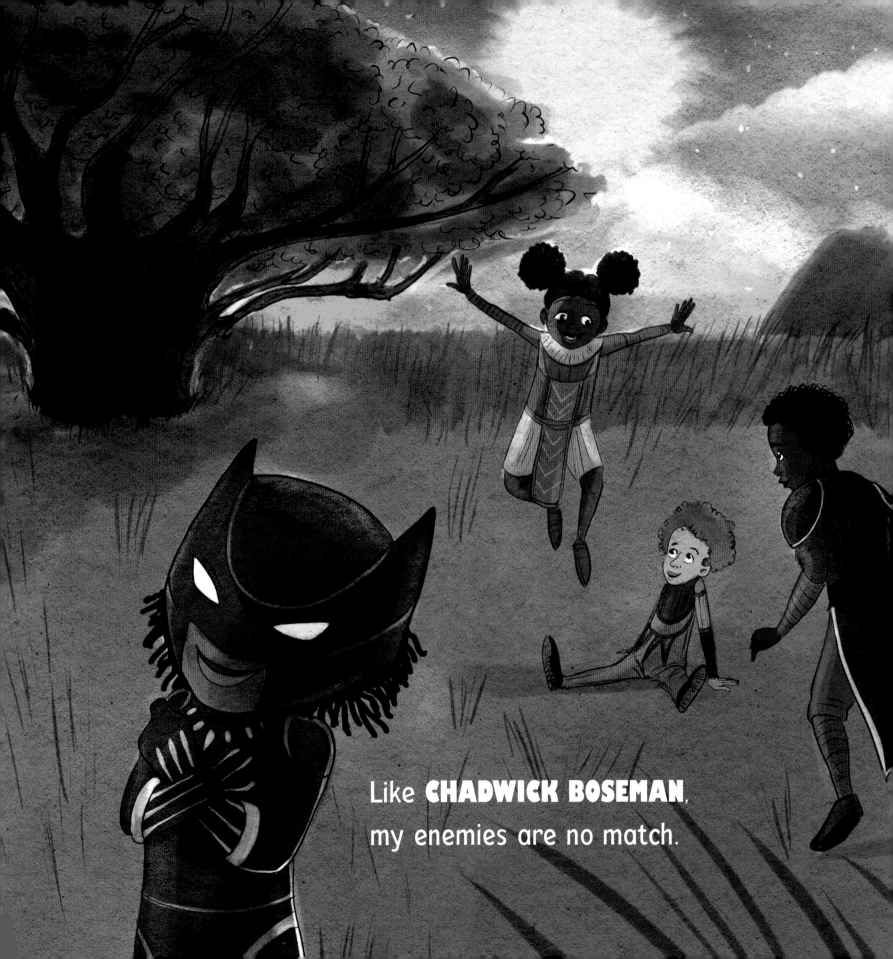

Like **CHADWICK BOSEMAN**,
my enemies are no match.

Whenever I ball,
and make the winning shot,
I channel my inner MAMBA,
my number 24,

my **KOBE BRYANT**,
my basketball HERO.

I AM my ancestors' wildest dreams.

Like **TUPAC** and **BIGGIE**,
I can use my VOICE to touch hearts
even when I'm young
and still growing.

I am NOT an invisible man.
People everywhere
will SEE ME like
RALPH ELLISON.

I'm the people's CHAMP,
like **MUHAMMAD ALI**.
Gentle like a butterfly,
my impact is STRONG like a bee.

And what if I want to start a bit of GOOD TROUBLE like **JOHN LEWIS**?

Or sit on the HIGHEST COURT like **THURGOOD MARSHALL**?

Student Council!

Or maybe I can do it ALL — play sports and still SAVE LIVES — like **DR. CHARLES DREW**.

"Life is a marathon,"
NIPSEY HUSSLE
used to say.
The race won't end
until I reach my DREAMS.

I AM my ancestors' wildest dreams.

I am ROYALTY.

I am LEGEND.

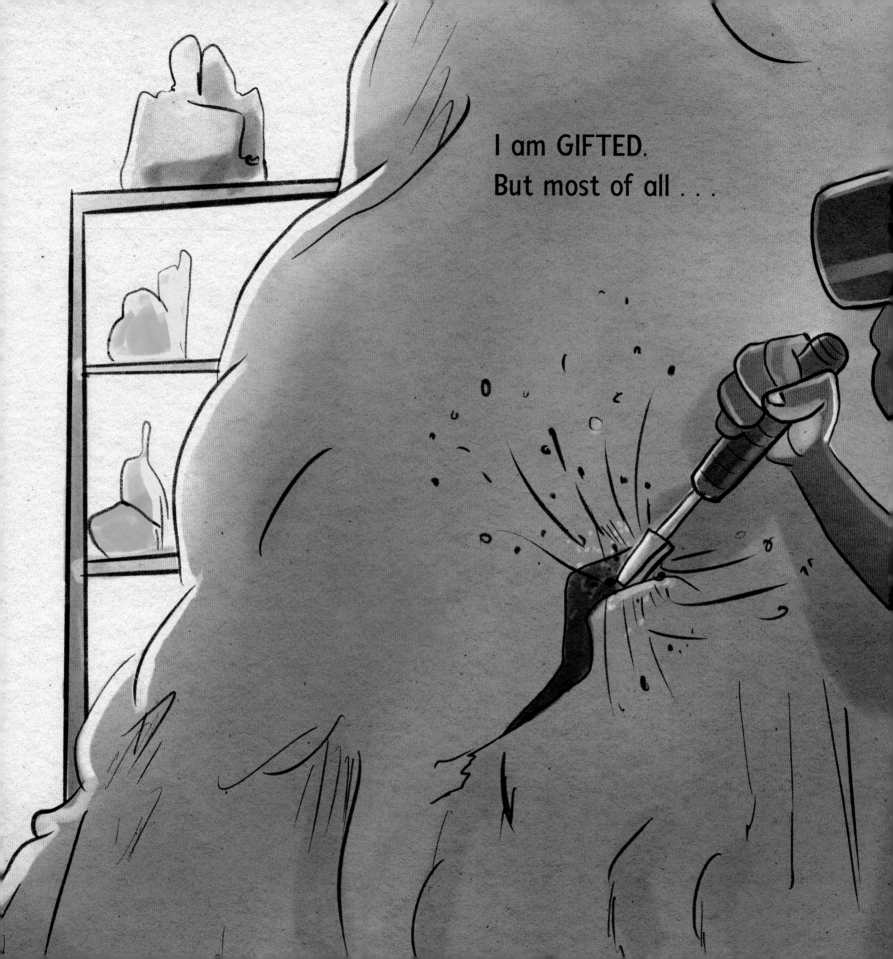

I AM my ancestors' wildest dreams.

A Note from the Author

Dear Reader,

Thank you for reading *I Am My Ancestors' Wildest Dreams*! At the time I wrote this book, Chadwick Boseman had just passed away a few days prior. He was so young but made such an impact during his short time on Earth. He was more than the iconic Black Panther — the character he played in the Marvel Universe — he was a husband, friend, gifted actor, creator, and philanthropist.

May this book serve as a reminder that you stand on the shoulders of historic giants like Representative John Lewis, Justice Thurgood Marshall, Dr. Charles Drew, and contemporary legends like Kobe Bryant and Nipsey Hussle. Use the men featured in this book as a starting point to learn more about others who have gone before and allow their stories to inspire you.

We often think we're too young, not smart enough, or lack the resources to make a difference. But you, my friend, can change the world! Even if you only reach one person. I hope you use all the talents given to you. May the legacy you leave behind be as beautiful, vibrant, and audacious as you are! Because someday you will be an ancestor, and someone will live out their wildest dreams because of YOU.

Be bold. Be brave. Be great.

I'm rooting for you,

xoxo Tee

A Little about These Ancestors

Chadwick Aaron Boseman (November 29, 1976–August 28, 2020): Chadwick Boseman was an actor, director, and playwright best known for his role in the Marvel Cinematic Universe as T'Challa in the movie *Black Panther*. Mr. Boseman was a hard worker and wasn't afraid to rise to challenges. "You want to choose a difficult way sometimes. Some days it should be simple, but sometimes you've got to take chances." Wakanda Forever.

Kobe Bean Bryant (August 23, 1978–January 26, 2020): Known as the "Black Mamba," Kobe Bryant was a philanthropist and an NBA All-Star, hailed as one of the most talented basketball players of all time. He once scored eighty-one points in one game! Off the court, Mr. Bryant hosted an annual basketball summer camp, and he and his wife partnered with an after-school program through the Kobe and Vanessa Bryant Family Foundation.

Tupac Shakur (June 16, 1971–September 13, 1996): Tupac Shakur was an actor, activist, lyricist, and one of the most influential rap artists of all time. Through writing poetry, his love for hip-hop grew. His albums have sold over seventy-five million copies, with *All Eyez on Me* garnering diamond status. He remains a symbol of activism against inequality.

Christopher "Notorious B.I.G." Wallace (May 21, 1972–March 9, 1997): The Notorious B.I.G., like Tupac, was one of the best lyricists of his generation and is considered one of the greatest rappers of all time. In 2020, he was inducted into the Rock & Roll Hall of Fame in the performers category. He often wrote and sang about his own life, the hard times and the uplifting ones.

 Ralph Ellison (March 1, 1914–April 16, 1994): Ralph Waldo Ellison was born in Oklahoma City, Oklahoma. As a child, he loved music and desired to be a classical music composer. He attended Tuskegee Institute, where he studied music and played the trumpet. In order to earn money for his last year of college, he traveled to New York City for work. There he met Langston Hughes and Richard Wright, who encouraged him to write. In 1952, he wrote *Invisible Man*, for which he won the National Book Award.

 Muhammad Ali (January 17, 1942–June 3, 2016): Formerly known as Cassius Marcellus Clay, Jr., Muhammad Ali was one of the greatest boxers of all time and is known as "The People's Champion" and "The Greatest." Mr. Ali had a big heart. He routinely traveled to foreign countries to help distribute medical supplies and lent a helping hand to orphanages.

 Supreme Court Justice Thurgood Marshall (July 2, 1908–January 24, 1993): Before becoming the first African American United States Supreme Court justice in 1967, Thurgood Marshall was a lawyer who argued thirty-two cases before the United States Supreme Court — the highest court in America — and won twenty-nine of them. He is best known for winning *Brown v. Board of Education of Topeka*, which made school segregation unconstitutional and allowed equal access to education for all children — because separate is not equal when it comes to education.

 Dr. Charles Richard Drew (June 3, 1904–April 1, 1950): Dr. Charles Drew was a surgeon and researcher who is known as the "Father of the Blood Bank." As a young person, he held many jobs, including paperboy, lifeguard, playground supervisor, and construction worker, before going to medical school. He is credited with creating a process to store and transport blood. His method is still used today by the American Red Cross.

 John Robert Lewis (February 21, 1940–July 17, 2020): A native of Troy, Alabama, John Lewis was a co-founder of the Student Nonviolent Coordinating Committee and became one of the original thirteen Freedom Riders. He served for over thirty years in Congress as an advocate for voting rights and is best known for helping to orchestrate a march in Selma, Alabama, to protest the blocking of Black Americans' right to vote.

 Ermias "Nipsey Hussle" Asghedom (August 15, 1985–March 31, 2019): Born in Crenshaw, California, and raised in South Central Los Angeles, Nipsey Hussle was a rapper, activist, and entrepreneur. In addition to being a talented artist, he consistently gave back to his community by helping to buy shoes for children, investing in the arts in Crenshaw, and creating a STEM center for inner city youth.

A Note from the Artist

To You, the beloved reader,

While illustrating *I Am My Ancestors' Wildest Dreams*, I concentrated on how the text made me feel. I meditated on colors, memories, emotions, and even the music that ascended from my soul. I wanted to take the reader on a journey that would help them feel at home with the narrative.

Love — that's what motivated these illustrations — my love for people, their individual stories, and for the lives I touch every day, regardless of the magnitude of my influence. Although some loved ones pass away, their love is always here to stay.

I hope this book cultivates inspiration and empowers young readers to dream, and dream BIG! Just as each of the influential Black men in this story began their journey with a dream imagined, I want to kindle imagination in each reader. Imagination is the seed of greatness.

— Robert

To Syd, Savvy, and Jay . . . each of you are my wildest dreams come true. — TM

To my Mama Rona. — RPJr.

Text Copyright © 2023 by Tanisia Moore • Art Copyright © 2023 by Robert Paul Jr. • All rights reserved. Published by Scholastic Press, an imprint of Scholastic Inc., *Publishers since 1920*. SCHOLASTIC, SCHOLASTIC PRESS, and associated logos are trademarks and/or registered trademarks of Scholastic Inc. • The publisher does not have any control over and does not assume any responsibility for author or third-party websites or their content. • No part of this publication may be reproduced, stored in a retrieval system, or transmitted in any form or by any means, electronic, mechanical, photocopying, recording, or otherwise, without written permission of the publisher. For information regarding permission, write to Scholastic Inc., Attention: Permissions Department, 557 Broadway, New York, NY 10012. • While inspired by real events and historical characters, this is a work of fiction and does not claim to be historically accurate or portray factual events or relationships. Please keep in mind that references to actual persons, living or dead, business establishments, events, or locales may not be factually accurate, but rather fictionalized by the author. • Library of Congress Cataloging-in-Publication Number: 2022004020 • ISBN 978-1-338-77617-1 • 10 9 8 7 6 5 4 3 2 1   23 24 25 26 27
Printed in China 38 • First edition, September 2023

Robert Paul Jr.'s art was digitally rendered with the use of scanned, cold pressed watercolor paper. Special care was taken to emulate watercolor paints and the smooth touch of creamy pastels. • The text type was set in Mingler Regular. • The display type was set in Gill Sans MT Pro Ultrabold Condensed. • The book was printed and bound at RR Donnelley Asia. • Production was overseen by Richard Gonzalez, Jr. • Manufacturing was supervised by Juliann Guerra. • The book was art directed and designed by Marijka Kostiw and edited by Tracy Mack.